W9-ATX-371

TALL BOY'S
Journey

by Joanna Halpert Kraus

illustrated by Karen Ritz

Carolrhoda Books, Inc. / Minneapolis

Dedicated to my husband, Ted, and to our son, Timothy Yang Kun

Text copyright © 1992 by Joanna Halpert Kraus
Illustrations copyright © 1992 by Carolrhoda Books, Inc.

This book is available in two editions:
Library binding by Carolrhoda Books, Inc.
Soft cover by First Avenue Editions
241 First Avenue North
Minneapolis, MN 55401

LIBRARY OF CONGRESS CATALOGING-IN-PUBLICATION DATA

Kraus, Joanna Halpert.
    Tall boy's journey / by Joanna Halpert Kraus : illustrations by Karen Ritz
        p.   cm
Summary: When Kim Moo Yong, a Korean orphan boy, is adopted by an American couple and makes the long journey by plane to their house, he finds it a strange and terrifying experience, until he begins to adjust to his new way of life.
    ISBN 0-87614-746-5 (lib. bdg.)
    ISBN 0-87614-616-7 (pbk.)
    [1. Korean Americans—Fiction. 2. Adoption—Fiction.] I. Ritz, Karen, ill. II. Title
PZ7.K8675Tal   1992
[Fic]—dc20
                                                                91-42326
                                                                   CIP
                                                                    AC

Manufactured in the United States of America

2 3 4 5 6 7 8 9 10 – P/JR – 01 00 99 98 97 96 95 94

Dear Reader,
    This book is
about my own son, Tim,
who arrived from Korea on a
giant jet when he was eight-and-
a-half years old. Through him
and the International
Adoption Group in
upstate New York, I met
other children who shared
their adoption experiences with me.
    All the events in this story really
happened, although not all to the same
person.
    This book is dedicated to my son
and to all adopted children and their
new families, who together will go
on their own journeys.
    Joanna H. Kraus

It was the day his whole class went hiking. It was the day his whole life changed.

All the third-grade students carried food for a picnic as they climbed high up into the Korean hills. Noodles, rice cakes, and seaweed. Cold spinach. Strawberries. It was a feast that left Kim Moo Yong breathless with contentment. When the last strawberry was gone, the children looked up and could see moving pictures in the clouds. Excitedly they pointed out ships and swords and the glorious battles of Korean heroes.

Then one boy brought out twelve colored marbles. The children forgot the blue sky above and concentrated on the glittering glass below.

"Whoever wins can keep them!" the boy announced. All afternoon Kim Moo Yong tried to win the orange-red one—the one that looked like leaping fire. And when he finally won, the children laughed and joked in admiration.

Kim Moo Yong held his prize marble tightly. When he held it up in the glow of the setting sun, it was even more beautiful. And he was sure, he was positive, that this would make his grandmother well. He ran home to give it to her, imagining her smile.

But when he saw the crowd of people at the door, his joy snapped like a young pine in the wind.

His Uncle Soo Ja, a soldier, stood there. "She would have liked to say good-bye to you," he said quietly.

No! He tried to push through the crowd. No! She couldn't leave him like that. Didn't she know he had won the marble for her?

Kim Moo Yong stopped eating. He refused his favorite noodle soup. He refused kimchi, the spicy cabbage that Koreans eat at every meal.

The whispers of the visitors stopped when he entered the house. But he caught snatches of what the villagers said to Uncle Soo Ja.

"No one. No one left. Who will take care of him?"

Kim Moo Yong knew that when he had been a baby his father had died. He couldn't remember him at all. But he remembered his mother, his ooma. On holidays when she wore the traditional long full skirt and short blouse with flowing sleeves, she seemed to float along the village path. Then her coughing began. She was like a fall flower cut down by harsh winds.

"So young. So sad," one of the villagers said. "Now this."

The next night, Kim Moo Yong threw the good noodle soup all over the floor. For a second, Uncle Soo Ja looked as though he would punish Kim Moo Yong. But instead he sighed, shook his head, and looked beyond the moon with his thoughts.

Kim Moo Yong didn't like all the whispers he heard. Why didn't Uncle Soo Ja scold him?

When he ran outside, no familiar voice called him back. No grandmother was there to say, "Come inside. A small boy makes a meal for a tiger."

The next day, a woman who was strange to the village came and talked with Uncle Soo Ja for an hour. "Orphan" was the word she kept repeating!

A sharp pain shot through Kim Moo Yong's stomach. He squatted on his heels, his head buried in his arms. He knew with a deep, dull ache that he would never see his mother again. He knew he would never thread the needle for his grandmother, his halmoni, or feel her fingers soothe his stomach when it hurt. He held the shirt she had sewed for him and sobbed.

Then Kim Moo Yong had an idea. He knew Uncle Soo Ja had to return to the army base far away. Kim Moo Yong tried on his military cap and paraded outside the house with a twig for a gun. Uncle Soo Ja would see what a splendid soldier he would make. But still Kim Moo Yong refused to eat. He had no taste for food.

The strange woman came again, one week later. She showed Kim Moo Yong a picture of a man and woman he had never seen before. She said they were Americans and would like to take care of him. Kim Moo Yong looked at the floor and refused to answer. The woman was crazy.

Right after she left, Uncle Soo Ja came in with a brown paper package. "Open it," he instructed.

Kim Moo Yong held his breath. He closed his eyes. He hoped it would be a soldier's uniform just like Uncle Soo Ja's. He would go with his uncle. He would polish his boots. He would help him. He would make Uncle Soo Ja proud. And he would be brave.

He tore off the string and opened the brown paper, his fingers trembling with excitement. But there was no soldier's cap inside. There was sturdy blue cloth, folded neatly. It was a little boy's jacket. Kim Moo Yong flung it on the floor.

"The army is no place for a boy," Uncle Soo Ja said, his dark eyes troubled. "I can't take you with me."

"But I want to be a soldier," Kim Moo Yong screamed, and the tears he had tried to hold back for days now fell thick and fast.

Uncle Soo Ja sat beside him and spoke as though he had memorized the words. "Kim Moo Yong, you need to eat well and grow strong. You need a mother and father to take care of you while you are growing. I can't take care of you. I'm a soldier. I have no home. Later, when you are older, you can come back."

Later? What did "later" mean?

Now Uncle Soo Ja's voice was soft and persuasive. "Kim Moo Yong, how would you like to go on a plane ride?"

What a question. He'd go anywhere with Uncle Soo Ja. "Where?" he asked. "Where?"

"All the way to America."

"With you?"

"No." Uncle Soo Ja looked at the boy beside him and then spoke gravely. "Kim Moo Yong, I am sending you on a mission. You are a Korean boy. You are brave, and I trust you."

"What do I have to do?" Kim Moo Yong asked. Now he was excited. He would help Uncle Soo Ja, whatever it was.

"You must eat. You must learn. You must grow."

"And that's all?" Kim Moo Yong demanded. "That's easy."

"No, it is not easy." Uncle Soo Ja corrected him sharply. "But when you have learned that it takes more courage to eat than to throw your soup on the floor, you will know what bravery means. You will be tall, inside. You will be Tall Boy. I said it was a difficult mission. But it is a mission for Ooma, for Halmoni, and for me. Will you be my soldier across the sea?"

Kim Moo Yong nodded.

"Then put the jacket on."

Dutifully, Kim Moo Yong obeyed.

Kim Moo Yong had never been on a plane before. He had never sped through skies, flown through storm clouds, watched dots become cars as the plane descended into cities he had never seen. He hardly slept. He raced the toy airplane the stewardess had given him. He saw the cockpit of the plane and imagined he was the pilot. He was a soldier for Uncle Soo Ja.

Day into dusk. Dusk into dawn. Seoul, Tokyo, Anchorage, Chicago. And then, as stars disappeared and snow covered the land below, New York.

The seat belt sign flashed on, and the plane began its descent into Kennedy Airport.

He remembered that the American man and woman had worn glasses in the photograph. No one in his entire village wore glasses. "In America they must have bad eyes," he concluded. Now he wondered if his eyes would spoil. As he thought about it, his hands began to perspire and his forehead was damp with fear.

The plane landed with a soft thud.

Now he and the other travelers were being led down a ramp into an enormous room. As he looked at the waiting crowd, he drew his breath in sharply. Their faces were white, like raw bean curd, and their noses were long and pointed. "They must get in the way of everything," he thought as he quickly touched his own flat nose.

Just then there was a flash. Instinctively, he fell to the ground and protected himself just the way Uncle Soo Ja had showed him. The floor was smooth and cold. When he looked up, people were laughing. A man with a red beard and glasses knelt down beside him and showed him a rectangular black box, where the flash had come from. Now a woman was kneeling beside him. Her hair was long, the color of a January sun when it shines through the clouds. Her face was the color of boiled rice except that across the nose were tiny brown flecks.

Kim Moo Yong stared at this peculiar creature. She wore a pink silk blouse, gray pants, and black boots. She did not resemble any woman he had ever seen before. Then it got worse. She put an arm lightly around his shoulders. He shrugged it off at once. Didn't

she know that you never hug a grown boy in public?

Suddenly he wondered if he would ever see Korean faces again. The thought made him dizzy. Immediately there was a swarm of white-faced adults speaking a language he couldn't understand. Their voices were loud and excited. One person tried to help him up. Another thrust a cold can in his face. Another pushed him back down. One put a red fruit in his hand.

Why didn't they all go away?

He wanted his own straw mat on the floor of his grandmother's home. Even the poorest house had a floor heated by the kitchen fires below, an ondul floor. If this new country was so rich, why was the floor so cold?

The man with the beard was wearing a blue jacket that looked like a quilt. From deep inside a pocket he pulled out a small, red wool hat. But when the man tried to put it on Kim Moo Yong's head, the boy flatly refused. He wasn't going to wear their clothes. Ever.

The man didn't seem upset. He grinned and firmly took Kim Moo Yong's hand. The woman with the long hair walked along with them.

As they made their way past crying babies, excited parents, and bored business travelers, Kim Moo Yong didn't want any of them to think he was scared. They made their way through the confusion of hundreds of different-sized suitcases and odd-shaped packages from cities all over the world. Kim Moo Yong wanted the man with the beard to know that he was strong and unafraid. He opened the glass exit door with a karate kick. It was a strong kick that rattled the glass. He looked up proudly. The man was whispering to the woman. They were both frowning.

Outside, a light snow was falling. The night was dark and starless. In the back of a small red car, the woman pushed something toward him. It was dark and furry. In the dim light of the road, Kim Moo Yong could just make out the shape of a small bear.

He screamed for his uncle.

"Ool-ji-ma," the woman murmured in Korean. "Don't cry." But he noticed that she didn't come too close to the bear either. She pretended not to see the tears that trickled silently down his face.

These people are crazy, he thought. They keep stuffed bears. I wonder what else they do? Maybe if I keep screaming, he told himself, they'll take me back. For an hour he screamed, until his throat was sore.

Finally the car stopped.

Relieved, Kim Moo Yong waited for them to turn the car around. But instead the man took him on his lap, and the woman slid behind the wheel. In his country, women didn't drive. Where were they going?

The car moved up the mountain road slowly. He peered out into the dark February night. On nights like this tigers came down from the mountain peaks and hunted for food. A tiger could easily break into this small car, this car that held the wild echo of the wind. He screamed in terror.

Two hours later, the car stopped in front of a two-story, white wooden house. From the street, a long flight of wooden steps led to a red door. The windows were made of glass instead of paper.

He thought of the home he'd just left, of the home where he'd been a baby and played under the thatched rice-straw roof.

He wondered if anyone ever laughed inside this giant house on the hill.

"I've decided I want to go home," Kim Moo Yong said politely in Korean. But they ignored him. "Take me back." This time his voice was urgent. "I want to go back!" The man and woman paused and murmured something Kim Moo Yong could not understand.

"Are you hungry?" the woman asked in halting Korean. The woman read the sentence from a thin, black book. Kim Moo Yong could barely understand her accent. He thought of the hot rice and kimchi he had eaten during his last day in the village and nodded. Just the memory of the spicy pickled cabbage made his eyes sting.

On a high wooden table he counted fifteen different kinds of food. He looked carefully. But there was nothing that looked like the kimchi that he had helped his grandmother make every autumn. The rice looked familiar. But when he tasted it, he spat it out. There was no comfort to this rice that was dry instead of moist, that was eaten with a fork instead of chopsticks. The metal banged his teeth, and he threw it on the floor. He had forgotten to bring the wooden chopsticks he'd carved himself. He knew just where they were too, beside his rice bowl that his grandmother had filled every day until the day she died. Hot tears stung his eyes at the memory of his grandmother.

"Oom-ma," the woman said pronouncing it carefully. She pointed to herself. "Oom-ma." Kim Moo Yong looked coldly at this woman who drove cars and wore pants and gave him rice with a fork. "Oom-ma!" How could she say such a word to him? She could never be his mother. Never!

She must have been angry, for she led him down a long corridor to another room, where her husband immediately pulled off Kim Moo Yong's Korean sweater and pants. The man motioned that he should climb into a low, blue tub filled with water. Kim Moo Yong understood that they wanted him to wash. At home he had used a barrel outside. Nervously, he put his

right foot in the blue tub. Then he howled in pain. What were they going to do to him? The water was hot! Not cold the way it should be. Hot water was for cooking! He knew he must run away. Better to be eaten by a mountain tiger than to be boiled alive by these crazy long-noses, who only pretended to smile.

After they added cold water to the bath, he splashed some over his tired body. He did not protest when she took a cloth and rubbed his face. He was busy planning his escape. The man smiled and lifted him from the tub, wrapping a huge towel around him. But Kim Moo Yong wasn't going to let a smile stop him.

The woman seemed to read his thoughts, for she began to sprinkle a fine white dust all over him. He thought it must be to prevent him from leaving. He felt himself getting tired in spite of his efforts to stay alert. She sang softly and rubbed his back gently. Was it magic?

"Uncle Soo Ja," he yelled. "Uncle Soo Ja!"

He was carried across the hall and put on a mattress high up in the air. In Korea he slept on his own mat on the floor. The boy felt his rage mounting. Never had he been punished like this, sent off to a separate room where he would have to spend the long night alone. Then he noticed the bear staring at him from the top of the bookcase.

The woman put the bear's face down so it could rest and indicated that Kim Moo Yong should do the same.

Kim Moo Yong decided he would leave that night. He closed his eyes and pretended to be asleep. But as soon as the man and woman left, he crept out of the room and tiptoed down the stairs. He found the red door and turned the knob.

It refused to open! Furious, he tried again. Maybe if he gave it a karate kick, it would open.

Suddenly a light clicked on. The man and woman stood there, watching.

Kim Moo Yong wondered if they would beat him. He was trapped. The door still wouldn't open. But he would not let them see he was afraid, no matter how they tortured him.

Now the woman took his hand, sat on the floor, and talked a language he could not understand. The man checked the door and then relocked it, adjusting the brass chain across the door frame. Kim Moo Yong carefully watched what the man did.

Then without a word, the man picked Kim Moo Yong up in his arms and carried him upstairs to a different room. There the bed looked big enough for six people. He put Kim Moo Yong down in the center, and the woman put a white, smooth cloth over his body and tucked it in. Kim Moo Yong kicked it off at once. Sighing, she took a soft quilt and placed it over him and tried to hold his hand. Kim Moo Yong jerked his hand loose. The man put his arm around her and led her out of the room.

Silences.

Unfamiliar smells.

He sat bolt upright in bed. Every wall in the room had pictures. Faces in frames. Ghosts staring out of painted eyes. He could not stay here. There was no time to lose. This time he knew what to do. He had watched the man unlock the door. Silently he slid the chain off, holding his breath, hoping they wouldn't hear him. Then he turned the snap lock, right to left, the opposite of what the man had done.

He opened the door. A cold gust of air surged through the hallway and knocked over a vase of flowers. Don't let them hear, Kim Moo Yong thought. Don't let them hear! He ran out of the house.

Within seconds, the man followed.

Kim Moo Yong stumbled on the unfamiliar stairs. Fresh snow fell across his thin jacket and covered his eyes. He fell. When the man picked him up from the ground, Kim Moo Yong's body was trembling with cold and fear. Now they had caught him.

"Oh, Richard!" Kim Moo Yong could hear the tears in the woman's voice. Satisfied that he hadn't been injured, the woman warmed his wind-chapped hands. From a bottle, she squeezed some white liquid into her own hands and rubbed it in. Kim Moo Yong watched fearfully. Then she put some on his hands and gently smoothed it on his fingers, across the backs of his hands, and into his palms. It was soft. It didn't hurt. He noticed that her eyes were blue and that the man called her Carolyn.

They did not beat him. The man and woman did not even look angry. But they placed him between them in their own bed. All night long they lay beside him. In the drowsy warmth that came toward dawn, he forgot to be frightened and fell asleep.

The next morning, Carolyn pointed in her thin, black book to the Korean word for breakfast. "A-cheem-bab," she said. Kim Moo Yong nodded. She showed him a picture of an egg in its shell and then pointed to a pan that held something yellow and fluffy. What was in the pan certainly didn't look like an egg to him! Kim Moo Yong shook his head. Then she offered him some water in a glass. Tentatively he tasted it, hoping it would not make him sick. By now he was more thirsty than hungry. He had a long way to go today.

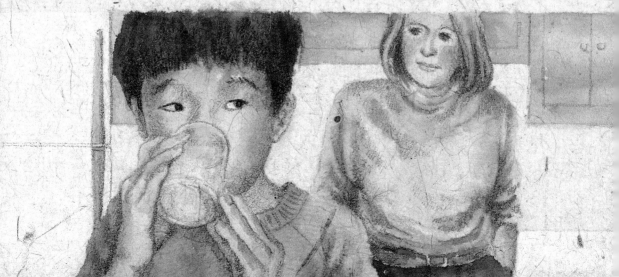

No sooner did he go outside than Richard came running after him. He tossed a rubber ball. Kim Moo Yong caught it and pointed to the car. Whistling, Richard unlocked it and began to demonstrate what the different buttons did. Kim Moo Yong had never seen so many gadgets, and he would have liked to try them all out. But he wasn't sure how long it would take to walk back to Korea. Impatiently, he interrupted.

"Please. Take me back. I want to go home now." Solemnly, he returned the rubber ball. He did not want them to say that he had taken anything of theirs. He said he was sorry about the vase, that it had been an accident. But Richard did not understand his Korean words.

Kim Moo Yong got out of the car and ran to the end of the street, where a small white dog began barking excitedly and chasing him. Kim Moo Yong hollered at it to go away. He waved his arms fiercely, but the dog jumped up and began to chew his jacket playfully. As Kim Moo Yong pulled away, he heard a loud rip. "Devil," he yelled in Korean. "Devil!"

Carolyn came running down the street. She spoke sharply to the dog, and it trotted away.

Kim Moo Yong wondered how many devils he'd have to pass before he reached home. Why didn't America have tall, thin spirit posts along the road? In Korea, stern eyes staring out from a carved wooden face at the top of a spirit post would always frighten devils away.

Now Carolyn turned Kim Moo Yong around to face a road he hadn't even noticed. Cars, trucks, buses, motorcycles all zoomed past in four directions. How many smooth roads did they have in this country? There had only been dirt roads near his village. A few times a day a truck or jeep would bump across. Sometimes he would steal a ride and boast to the other children. But these cars were moving too fast for him to hang on. Which way should he go? It wasn't going to be easy to get back to Korea. He would need help.

Back at the house, Richard was talking to a tall Korean man. Kim Moo Yong didn't know there were any other Koreans here. He bowed as was customary for boys to do before the men in the village. But why did this man wear American-style shoes inside the house?

Familiar Korean words bathed his ears, a melody first sweet, then sour. "Your new family . . . wants you . . . an opportunity . . . try not to spoil it," said this man whose name was Mr. Cho.

Sullenly Kim Moo Yong stared at the floor. He was not going to stay in a country where he might starve—a country without kimchi.

As if in answer to his thought, Mr. Cho walked calmly into the kitchen, turned a knob, and waited for the blue flame to spring up. "How did you do that?" Kim Moo Yong asked, amazed at what he saw.

Mr. Cho smiled. "Americans don't realize how extraordinary their kitchens are! When you learn to speak English, you'll have to tell your new mother how you scrambled for dry wood each day to feed the kitchen fire."

"How did you know about that?" asked Kim Moo Yong.

"I did the same," Mr. Cho replied as he opened a plain paper bag with a flourish. Kimchi!

Kim Moo Yong felt hungry just smelling the familiar cabbage and hot spices. Kim Moo Yong ate and held up his bowl for more.

After three bowls of noodles and two bowls of kimchi, he felt better. He noticed Carolyn looked happy too.

"I think you were hungry," Mr. Cho stated. "When did you eat last?"

"Just before I left," said Kim Moo Yong.

Mr. Cho was startled. "That was three days ago."

"I know," he said as he gestured to Carolyn and Richard. "I was afraid their food might poison me. How long will it take me to walk back?"

Mr. Cho looked solemn and took Kim Moo Yong back into the room with the high bed, the bookshelves, and the bear. On the wall was a large world map. Carefully he traced Kim Moo Yong's journey. There were oceans to swim and continents to cross. When Kim Moo Yong understood that he could never walk home, he sank down on his knees and his forehead touched the alien carpet. His shoulders shook, but he made no sound.

"This is your new home," Mr. Cho said gently.

"No!" Kim Moo Yong spat out. "No!"

After a while Mr. Cho spoke again.

"In my father's house, my grandfather would gather all the children in the late afternoon and tell us stories of old Korea. He always began the same way. 'Children, it is true we don't have many coins, but we do have lots of stories.' And we would all laugh and sit beside him and listen.

Sometimes, if we were very quiet, he would tell us stories until the first star appeared."

Kim Moo Yong squatted on the floor and looked up expectantly at Mr. Cho, who was looking out the window at a time long past and was remembering people long gone.

Slowly his voice began to unwrap memories. He told Kim Moo Yong the story of Yi Sun-shin, the naval hero whose boat had baffled and beaten the enemy during the fifteenth century.

"I know all about him," said Kim Moo Yong. "We learned about him at school." Mr. Cho looked at him intently.

"Then now," he said, "you must learn to be as brave as Yi Sun-shin, in your new country."

"But if I don't go back," Kim Moo Yong blurted out, "all my friends will forget me."

Mr. Cho listened as if he remembered that fear. "Maybe you could draw a picture of your new home and your new room and send it to them."

"My room? Where?" he asked in surprise.

"Here! Right here! This is your room. You can study here, sleep here, and play here."

This! This was his room? But it couldn't be. It had no heated floor, no low table for eating, no sleeping mat. Instead there was a strange, high bed with bright pillows that had buttons in the middle. He looked at the hanging green plant and the painted white walls. "I don't like this room," he said flatly.

Then Kim Moo Yong pointed to the bear. "What's that?"

Mr. Cho looked at him surprised and then laughed. "It's a toy, a teddy bear." He picked it up. "Although this one looks almost real."

"I never had a toy before," Kim Moo Yong said matter-of-factly. He was positive he'd never play with this one, either.

"Most American children want one."

"Well, I'm not American," he retorted hotly. "I'm a Korean." Still he was curious. "Why do they want one?"

"A teddy bear is a friend."

"A friend!" The idea was absurd.

"A friend who listens to you, a friend who never disagrees with you, and a friend who never gets angry," Mr. Cho said with a twinkle.

"Oh," the boy said.

"But we can tell your mother you don't like it," said Mr. Cho.

Kim Moo Yong winced at the word "mother."

"Your American mother," Mr. Cho corrected himself casually. "Or you can put it away for a while."

Kim Moo Yong touched the bear's arms with the toe of his shoe. Nothing happened. Why was it everything in this country made him feel foolish? "Well, it can stay. For a while," he said as he pointed to the shelf on the far side of the room. "Over there."

Then he asked the question that bothered him most. "Why do they have such a large house?" Kim Moo Yong whispered. "They have two places to eat, one where I had the kimchi and where you made the fire. But there's another room. It has a long brown table with eight chairs. I counted them. And they have two indoor bathrooms. With hot water. When are all the other people coming?"

"There are no other people," Mr. Cho replied.

"With all these rooms? There must be!" said Kim Moo Yong.

"No. Just the three of you," said Mr. Cho.

"Aren't you going to live here either?" asked the boy.

"No. I just work with your father. In the same laboratory. We're both scientists," said Mr. Cho. "But I'll come back, and I'll bring more kimchi tomorrow."

"I was just learning how to read," Kim Moo Yong complained, "when I had to come to

America. My Uncle Soo Ja said, 'It's a wonderful country. Just wait and see.' "

Mr. Cho smiled thoughtfully. "In some ways it is. Why don't you wait and see."

"There's no place as beautiful as Korea. No place!" Kim Moo Yong insisted.

"A boy who has traveled through the earth's skies, over different seas, may have more than one home in his heart."

But Kim Moo Yong wasn't paying attention to Mr. Cho. The young boy heard only the loneliness inside. He said, "I don't like long noses. When she tries to speak Korean, all she does is read words from a book, and she doesn't pronounce them right. I can't even tell if she's talking Korean or American."

"It's called English," Mr. Cho said firmly. "And you'll have to learn it, just as I did when I came."

"I had lots of friends in Korea." Kim Moo Yong looked down at the floor, as though he could look through the earth and imagine them all playing on the other side without him. "Lots!"

"You need some children to play with." Mr. Cho rose and went out.

All the next day and into the evening, snow fell. By the time it stopped, it was two feet high. Not a footprint had disturbed it yet. Icicles clung to the tree branches, and the hill sparkled in the sunrise. A boy about Kim Moo Yong's age arrived at the front door, his cheeks glowing from the cold. He talked to Carolyn, who looked glad to see him.

"Hi!" he said to Kim Moo Yong. "I'm Scott." He carried a blue plastic toboggan and pointed to the nearby hill. Carolyn put out a warm jacket that looked just like Richard's except that it was Kim Moo Yong's size.

"C'mon," Scott said excitedly. "If we hurry, we'll be the first ones there!" In a few minutes Kim Moo Yong was behind him, speeding down

a frosty hill. They shrieked happily as they barely missed a tree stump.

Soon other children came to the hill with sleds and skis. But no one, no one, had a toboggan like this one.

After a few runs, Scott said, "Now it's your turn. You steer." He gestured that Kim Moo Yong should sit in front. Oh, if the boys in his village could see him now. They loved to move fast, to race with the wind. Kim Moo Yong would have liked to talk to this boy, this boy with a big grin, who made tobogganing so much fun.

Soon another group came with a red toboggan, and they raced them down the hill, ending in a heap at the bottom. All of them were laughing.

Then Scott lay on his back and flapped his arms. When he got up, there was an angel in the snow. The other children happily copied

Scott's idea, and soon Kim Moo Yong was lying on his back flapping his arms and laughing with them.

Then, all the way up the long hill Scott walked in Kim Moo Yong's footsteps. Kim Moo Yong made his steps longer and longer, then wider and wider. He kept turning around, but Scott didn't miss once. He just grinned and waved. They sped down the hill in seconds, and this time Scott ran up the hill first, leaping, jumping, and occasionally walking. Kim Moo Yong followed his footsteps exactly.

It was strange how you could understand someone even though you couldn't speak his language.

They were very wet and still giggling when they got back to Kim Moo Yong's house.

From the kitchen stove came the delicious smell of hot turkey soup cooking. Kim Moo

Yong and Scott each had two bowls and half of a box of round salty crackers. Kim Moo Yong sighed contentedly. His stomach was warm and full.

Kim Moo Yong improvised skis out of sticks, the way he had made them in Korea, and he taught Scott how to whiz down the hill. Afterwards Scott taught him how to make popcorn in a frying pan. It still startled Kim Moo Yong just to turn a knob and have a flame appear, but he kept that thought to himself.

Mr. Cho came often, bringing fresh bean curd or soy sauce or Korean picture books. Kim Moo Yong listened to Mr. Cho's musical voice, but afterward he would stare out the window and gaze at mountains that no one else could see.

One night Kim Moo Yong gave Carolyn and Richard a lesson in how to eat with chopsticks. They all laughed as Carolyn triumphantly held up a piece of meat. Later Mr. Cho and Kim Moo Yong sang Korean songs.

But then it was bedtime. Kim Moo Yong confided to Mr. Cho, "The daytime goes fast. But ... ," his voice faltered. "I wish the night ... were daytime. In Korea I played outside as long as I liked. I went to bed with the adults." As if to make himself braver, Kim Moo Yong began telling Mr. Cho how they hid behind the trees. "Sometimes we made ghost sounds. Sometimes we'd tell ghost stories. But I was never scared." He looked up the dark staircase that led to his room and hesitated. In Korea no one ever had to sleep alone. "Why can't I sleep with them? What do I do," he whispered, "if a tiger comes in the middle of the night?"

In Kim Moo Yong's room, Carolyn spoke softly to Mr. Cho. Kim Moo Yong could tell she was talking about him. "He doesn't want to sleep in his own room. He's frightened, I guess. Every night he gets up and comes to our room."

Mr. Cho looked thoughtfully at Kim Moo Yong and said to him, "Why don't you keep a big stick by your bed to beat the tigers and make them go away."

"When I was a child," he told Carolyn and Richard, "my grandfather warned me about tigers coming down from the mountains. He warned us to stay inside on moonless nights. Your son has heard those stories too. Sometimes tigers did come down from the mountains to the village. I told him to keep a tiger stick. I think he'll sleep better."

"But there are no wild animals here!" Richard said.

"How does he know that?" Carolyn answered. She promptly got the broom and put it beside Kim Moo Yong's bed.

As the first star appeared, Mr. Cho sat beside Kim Moo Yong and read a story from a Korean book that had long belonged to him. Now he was giving it to Kim Moo Yong. The pictures were bright and colorful. Eagerly, Kim Moo Yong pointed out different objects. He taught Carolyn and Richard, seated on large floor cushions, the correct Korean names. They had trouble saying some of the words, but as they practiced, Kim Moo Yong nodded his approval.

Finally, Kim Moo Yong yawned. Carolyn quietly put out the light and sat beside him. Mr. Cho tiptoed out. When Carolyn kissed him good night on the forehead, Kim Moo Yong was surprised that the point of her nose did not hurt at all.

Richard reached over and squeezed Kim Moo Yong's hand tightly. Sleepily, Kim Moo Yong wondered if his own hands would ever be that large.

His eyes closed slowly.

And the tigers stayed respectfully beyond the bedroom door.